DIRKLE SMAT
INSIDE MOUNT FLATBOTTOM

Lynn Garthwaite

Inside
Mount Flatbottom

LYNN D. GARTHWAITE

Illustrated by Craig Howarth

CASTLE KEEP PRESS
James A. Rock & Company, Publishers
Rockville, Maryland

Dirkle Smat Inside Mount Flatbottom by Lynn D. Garthwaite
Illustrated by Craig Howarth

CASTLE KEEP PRESS

CASTLE KEEP PRESS
is an imprint of JAMES A. ROCK & CO., PUBLISHERS

Dirkle Smat Inside Mount Flatbottom
copyright ©2006 by Lynn D. Garthwaite

Special contents of this edition copyright ©2006
by James A. Rock & Co., Publishers

Address comments and inquiries to:
CASTLE KEEP PRESS
James A. Rock & Company, Publishers
9710 Traville Gateway Drive, #305
Rockville, MD 20850

E-mail:
jrock@rockpublishing.com   lrock@rockpublishing.com
Internet URL: www.rockpublishing.com

EAN: 978-1-59663-512-8 / ISBN 1-59663-512-6

Library of Congress Control Number: 2006924408

Printed in the United States of America

First Edition 2006

Cover and interior illustrations by Craig Howarth
http://home.wol.co.za/~20291447/

Also in this series:
Dirkle Smat and the Flying Statue
Dirkle Smat and the Viking Shield

Check out Fun Stuff at
www.dirklesmat.com

To Brian, Ryan and Scott

*Thanks for the support
and the laughs.*

Chapter One

When Dirkle Smat stubbed his toe in the morning he had no idea that it would later save his life. Saturday started out with a sore toe, hair so mussed by the pillow that the wettest comb wouldn't make it stay flat, and a kid brother who ate the last of the Crinkly Flakes.

With his injured toe wrapped like a little mummy, Dirkle sprawled on the couch feeling sorry for himself. He tried to amuse himself writing code words on a mini-notepad, but for once his spy master brain just wasn't working.

Frustrated, he pocketed the pen and notepad and hopped on his bike. If he had been at his super spy sharpest and had a stomach full of Crinkly Flakes, he probably would have noticed his brother Quid following on his bike a hundred yards behind.

The members of the Explorers Club had agreed to meet at Fiddy Bublob's house to plan their day. Fiddy lived next to a pond and a woods filled with things to investigate, so the Explorers Club spent much of their time there. A couple of days before, Dirkle and fellow Explorer Bean Lumley had discovered the opening to a tunnel at the base of Mount Flatbottom, and today was the day to find out what was inside.

Dirkle spotted Toonie Oobles and Fiddy climbing a tree by the pond. Bean pulled in alongside him on his roto-scooter as Dirkle stepped off his bike. Bean always had a new invention, and the roto-scooter was his newest form of transportation.

"You're a genius Bean" said Dirkle in awe. "That thing would have helped me today with only nine toes for peddling."

Bean and Dirkle looked up to see Quid skid to a stop behind them.

"Hey, Bean," said Quid. "What did you do to your bike?"

"I call it a roto-scooter," said Bean. "I assumed you'd be joining us, Quid," he said matter-of-factly. "I fabricated an extra BL2 Helmet just in case."

"What's a BL2 Helmet?" Dirkle asked, as Toonie and Fiddy jumped down from the tree and joined the group.

"It's a 'Bean Lumley Second Generation' version of my cave explorer's helmet. The

first version kept failing to work, so I discarded it and came up with version two. The secret is in the hinge joints which allow wearers to shine the light at whatever angle they choose. Here, try them on."

The gang watched as Bean reached into his carrier and pulled out five bike helmets with flashlights mounted on the top.

"Extra batteries are built right into the back of the helmets. Life expectancy — four hours."

Fiddy gulped when he realized they might really be going through with this. "Four hours, huh? That should about do it . . . I suppose." He looked at the faces of his friends who were nodding quietly.

"With the helmets ready, we can explore the cave today," Dirkle said with satisfaction. "Fiddy, you said you'd supply the grub. What kind of sandwiches are you making?"

"Baloney and olive, with Swiss cheese."

"All right, my favorite!" said Quid appreciatively.

Chapter Two

Half an hour later, the five were assembled at the entrance to the cave. Fiddy had a backpack filled with sandwiches, Toonie had a gallon water bottle strapped to her back, Bean passed out helmets to everyone, and Quid looked back one last time at daylight before they pushed aside the brush to reveal the small opening in the side of the mountain.

Fifty yards into the tunnel, having for-

gotten to limp for sympathy, Dirkle stopped short.

"We've got a choice guys. This tunnel splits off in two directions. How do we know which way to go?"

Quid spoke up, his voice sounding more brave than he felt. "I'll walk in the left tunnel for about 30 steps. If it looks like it leads anywhere, I'll call for you to join me. If it looks like a dead end I'll come back here and we'll take the right."

They all looked at each other and nodded. It sounded like a good plan, and Fiddy was happiest with the part that let him stay in one place while Quid explored. They were nervous watching him go, but smiled with relief when he reappeared a few minutes later.

"Dead end," he reported. "The tunnel gets so low that we couldn't possibly squeeze through there."

"Then let's take the right tunnel and keep moving," Dirkle said like a leader.

Chapter Three

The Explorers were grateful for the strong lights from their BL2 helmets. Between the five of them they lit up the tunnel like a living room. They looked for any sign that other people had been in the tunnel, but the walls were bare and cold and the floor of the tunnel was uneven and rocky. After another twenty minutes they were getting tired of walking on the rough floor and Dirkle finally spoke up.

"I think it's time to take a break. Let's have one of those baloney and olive sandwiches, Fiddy. And we'll all have a ration of water too."

"I think it would be a prudent idea if half of us shut off our helmet lights temporarily to save battery power," reported Bean. Quid and Toonie obligingly shut off their lights, and Dirkle shut off one side of his. The tunnel instantly felt much more gloomy with only half the light, and the gang ate their lunch in silence, not eager to hear the echo of their voices.

"What do you think we'll find at the end of the tunnel?" Fiddy asked nervously.

"Possibly nothing," replied Bean. "But then again, perhaps an important scientific discovery."

"Maybe a gold mine," piped in Toonie, her face lit up with anticipation.

"Or maybe a spectacular underground waterfall," offered Quid, listening ahead to see if he could hear it.

"It's entirely possible the tunnel just goes right through and out the other side of the mountain. If that's the case, we may have a long walk ahead of us," Dirkle said almost to himself.

"And if that's the case, I don't think I made enough sandwiches," pouted Fiddy.

When it was time to start moving again, the crew picked up their mess and switched all lights back on. Within minutes they had come to another problem.

"The tunnel forks again," said Dirkle. "But this time there are three choices."

The five groaned as they considered the situation. Dirkle pulled out the mini notepad and pen that he had stuck in his pocket that morning and made a decision.

"I'm going to make a map. I'll draw the tunnel with all of the forks that we come to and that way we'll be able to retrace our steps when we return. The Explorers have never gotten lost, and we're not about to start now."

Half an hour later, after many twists and turns and three more forks in the tunnel, Toonie grabbed Dirkle's arm and stopped.

"Shh," she said. "Do you hear that?"

Everyone stopped to listen, and sure enough there were sounds ahead in the tunnel.

"Are those voices?" whispered Fiddy.

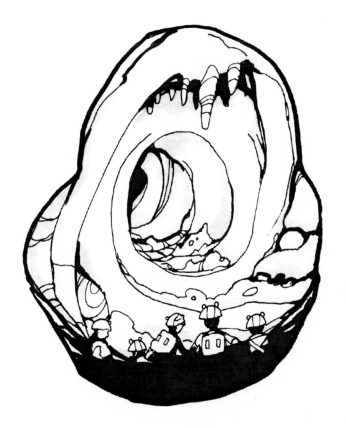

"Maybe a radio," suggested Quid.

"Either way, it means someone's up ahead in the tunnel," Dirkle said, not feeling quite as brave as he sounded.

"What if they're coming this way?" asked Toonie. "There's no place to hide!"

The group listened quietly for a moment while deciding what to do.

"It doesn't sound like the voices are getting any closer," whispered Dirkle. "I say we go ahead, but walk very, very quietly."

For several minutes they walked very slowly, held their breath, and tried as hard as they could to not make any sound at all. The tunnel was getting lighter and lighter and they could tell that things were brightly lit up ahead. The light was so bright that they could turn off their BL2 Helmet lights.

What they finally saw when they turned the corner made them gasp.

Chapter Four

"Yoips!" said Dirkle, because he was startled.

The tunnel ended at the entrance to a gigantic cave, almost the size of the domed stadium where they watched their favorite football team. The ceiling was at least four stories high and the room was lit by some kind of huge lights hanging from the roof. The massive room seemed to be divided into separate areas by partial walls, as if there were lots of rooms of all sizes.

And walking all around, reading, or sitting in chairs talking with each other . . . were people.

But not *really* people, at least not ones that looked like Dirkle and his friends. They were really, really tall, perhaps 7 or 8 feet tall, and they were covered with long, silky hair. Some were light haired, some had dark hair, but they all had hair from the top of their heads all the way down to their toes.

"It's Bigfoot!" whispered Bean. "A plethora of Bigfoots."

"What's Bigfoot?" asked Fiddy, although he was beginning to think he already knew.

"It's supposed to be just a legend, like the Loch Ness Monster, or Paul Bunyan," Dirkle told him.

"Some people claim they've seen these big, hairy ape-like people, but no one ever believes them," added Toonie. "Do you guys think we're dreaming?"

Suddenly a voice startled them.

"Who are you?"

Someone had quietly walked up to the tunnel entrance where they were hiding and was speaking to them. The Explorers all turned to see a tiny version of the hairy people, no bigger than they were, looking at them curiously.

19

They all stared at him, and he smiled back.

"Hi. My name is Fonny. You're from the outside, aren't you?"

Dirkle was the first to speak up.

"Yeah, I guess we are. We came through the tunnel under the mountain. What are you all doing here?" He pointed to the other Bigfoots walking around.

"We live here," answered Fonny. "This is our cave and these are my family and friends," he said proudly.

Bean cleared his throat. "Every once in a while, someone in our world reports a sighting of one of your . . . family. Do some of them come out of the cave sometimes?"

Fonny looked a little embarrassed. "I guess it's true, they do. They're not supposed to. Our laws say that we're supposed to keep to ourselves and not mingle with the outside people, but sometimes someone just gets so curious that they wander out there."

"And then someone spots them and takes a picture!" exclaimed Toonie. But by the time others come to see, the Bigfoot is gone."

"We don't call ourselves Bigfoot," answered Fonny. "We're Taymian, and there are other Taymian people in different parts of the world. We've been talking about organizing a big reunion one of these days, but no one can agree on where to hold it."

"So you never go outside?" asked Fiddy.

"Never see the sun?" added Quid.

"We have certain days that we're allowed to go out in small groups," said Fonny. "But we never go far from the tunnel entrance. I always think it's too bright and I can't wait to come back to the cave."

"I guess people usually just prefer what they're used to," Dirkle said wisely.

"Can we look around?" asked Fiddy.

Fonny was excited to show off his home to the visitors. They took a tour through the main gathering area and got a few stares from the other Taymian who were there. Fonny showed them his own home where he lived with his family. Each family had a space at the side of the cave where the cave wall formed the back of the house and three other walls were built for privacy. There was no door though, and nothing anywhere was locked up.

"Aren't you afraid of having something stolen?" asked Toonie.

"What does 'stolen' mean?" Fonny asked, his face curious.

Bean spoke up. "That's when someone takes something that doesn't belong to them."

Fonny shrugged. "Why would anyone do that? We all have everything we need, and if something gets broken, you just go to the group storeroom and get another one. Everything is shared."

Dirkle looked at his friends and smiled. "That sounds like a pretty cool way to live!"

The tour continued to an oversized tunnel off to one side. Inside were huge lamps on the ceiling, and fruits and vegetables of all kinds were growing in large dirt basins.

"We all take turns caring for the garden," said Fonny. "My family will be in charge of it next, and we take great pride in keeping it healthy so we have plenty to eat."

Another side cave, just as big as the main cave, appeared to be a large play area, with bases marked in some kind of cave version of baseball, and other roped off sections with goals and seating areas.

"We're starting our Rumjah tournament soon, and the winning team leads the parade to the feast," reported Fonny.

The Explorers stared in awe at all they were seeing. It was like a mini-city under the mountain! They saw a magnificent waterfall, a large natural pool with several Taymian swimming in it, colorful wall hangings everywhere that brightened up the cave walls and happy, smiling Taymian everywhere they turned.

Although Fonny's people were curious about the visitors, no one appeared either afraid or angry that they were there.

Suddenly one of Toonie's BL2 Helmet lights blinked on and off.

Chapter Five

"The batteries continue draining a bit, even when the lights are turned off," reported Bean with his usual efficiency. "We're going to have to switch to our back-up batteries soon, which means we better turn around and go back."

"I don't want to leave yet!" wailed Fiddy. "This is too cool!"

"Maybe you can come back another day," suggested Fonny.

"I don't think that would be too smart," said Toonie. "If anyone ever followed us, your secret would be out and you'd never be left alone."

Her friends nodded.

"She's right," said Quid. "If anyone else from our world found out about this cave, they'd be here with cameras and reporters and tourists . . . and you'd never have another quiet moment."

The Explorers looked at each other and all agreed. The Taymian people were going to have to be their secret forever.

Bean explained to Fonny that their lights would only last so long and they had to get back to make sure they could see their way through the tunnel before the batteries ran out. They all said good-byes to Fonny and thanked him for showing them around.

"If you ever need anything from us, just come to the mouth of the tunnel and hang this out for us to see," said Dirkle, handing

Fonny his lucky red kerchief. "We'll place some weeds over the entrance to the tunnel so no one else will get back here, but you'll be able to get past them to hang this up."

Fonny thanked him and said he hoped they'd see each other soon.

And so, reluctantly, the Explorers turned back into the tunnel they'd come through and headed back to find home.

But part way into the tunnel, they started to panic.

"Here's one of those forks in the road!" cried Toonie. "How do we know which way is the right way?"

"My map" said Dirkle calmly. "Remember? I used my notepad to draw a map of every turn we made."

He pulled out his notepad and studied it for a minute.

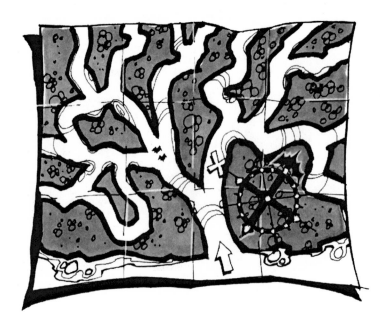

"This way," he pointed, showing the gang the left-hand corridor.

"Are you sure?" asked Quid.

"Yep. My maps are always right-on accurate," said Dirkle, and he confidently led the way through the tunnel.

Five more times they came to twists and turns and forks in the tunnel, and each time Dirkle's map showed them exactly the way to go.

But they wondered if they'd get back in time. One by one the back-up batteries were giving out and the BL2 Helmet lights were sizzling and losing power. Soon they were huddled together, barely able to see each other because only one light on Quid's helmet and one light on Toonie's helmet were still working. Dirkle used Quid's helmet light to see his map and bravely pushed on, feeling his way along the walls as well as he could.

When they finally reached the mouth of the tunnel, everyone gave a great sigh of relief because they had started to lose that Explorer confidence. They were minutes away from losing all light and they knew it.

"Yoips," said Dirkle, because he was relieved.

"Your map saved our lives," said Toonie.

"Yeah, I guess it did," answered Dirkle. "Who would have guessed that a stubbed toe would save someone's life? It was only because I was resting my toe that I had this notebook with me."

"I wish we could visit Fonny again," said Quid quietly. "I'd like to learn more about the Taymian."

"I know what you mean, but we can't take that risk," answered Toonie.

"If we don't leave them alone, there's a chance that others will find out about them," said Bean. "And that would be the end of them."

"But we know the secret to the Bigfoot mystery!" said Fiddy.

"And it'll have to stay our secret," said Dirkle. "Maybe someday they'll come out on their own and introduce themselves to our world. But that has to be their choice."

And the Explorers loaded up their gear, got on their bikes, and headed for home. It was almost dinner time and they needed to rest up for the next adventure!

About
the Author

Lynn Garthwaite lives in Bloomington, Minnesota with her husband and two sons. Neither of her sons is named Dirkle.

Make Your Own Explorer's Club

Members:

_____

_____

_____

_____

_____

Members:

_____

_____

_____

_____

_____

Equipment:

_____

_____

_____

_____

_____

_____

Adventures:

_____

_____

_____

_____

_____

_____

CPSIA information can be obtained at www.ICGtesting.com
Printed in the USA
BVOW07s2132270813

329288BV00001B/12/P